W9-DGS-847

About the Bank Street Ready-to-Read Series

More than seventy-five years of educational research, innovative teaching, and quality publishing have earned The Bank Street College of Education its reputation as America's most trusted name in early childhood education.

Because no two children are exactly alike in their development, the Bank Street Ready-to-Read series is written on three levels to accommodate the individual stages of reading readiness of children ages three through eight.

- ***Level 1:*** **Getting Ready to Read (Pre-K–Grade 1)**
  Level 1 books are perfect for reading aloud with children who are getting ready to read or just starting to read words or phrases. These books feature large type, repetition, and simple sentences.
- ***Level 2:*** **Reading Together (Grades 1–3)**
  These books have slightly smaller type and longer sentences. They are ideal for children beginning to read by themselves who may need help.
- ***Level 3:*** **I Can Read It Myself (Grades 2–3)**
  These stories are just right for children who can read independently. They offer more complex and challenging stories and sentences.

All three levels of The Bank Street Ready-to-Read books make it easy to select the books most appropriate for your child's development and enable him or her to grow with the series step by step. The levels purposely overlap to reinforce skills and further encourage reading.

We feel that making reading fun is the single most important thing anyone can do to help children become good readers. We hope you will become part of Bank Street's long tradition of learning through sharing.

The Bank Street College of Education

For Matt Hickey
—E.C., D.O., and E.S.

To Haley from Frank and Rosie
—R.B.M.

SHE'LL BE COMING AROUND THE MOUNTAIN

A Bantam Book/September 1994

Published by Bantam Doubleday Dell Books for Young Readers, a division of Bantam Doubleday Dell Publishing Group, Inc. 1540 Broadway, New York, New York 10036.

Series graphic design by Alex Jay/Studio J
Associate Editor: Kathy Huck

Special thanks to Betsy Gould, Susan Schwarzchild, and Matt Hickey.

The trademarks "Bantam Books" and the portrayal of a rooster are registered in the U.S. Patent and Trademark Office and in other countries. Marca Registrada.

Library of Congress Cataloging-in-Publication Data

Coplon, Emily.
She'll be coming around the mountain /
by Emily Coplon, Doris Orgel, and Ellen Schecter ;
illustrated by Rowan Barnes-Murphy.
p. cm.—(Bank Street ready-to-read)
"A Byron Preiss book."
Summary: This new version of the song "She'll Be Coming Around the Mountain" depicts a boisterous family celebration.
ISBN 0-553-09044-5 (hardcover).—ISBN 0-553-37340-4 (pbk.)
1. Children's songs—Texts. [1. Songs.]
I. Orgel, Doris. II. Schecter, Ellen.
III. Barnes-Murphy, Rowan, ill. IV. Title.
V. Title: She'll be coming around the mountain.
VI. Series.
PZ8.3.C8Sh 1994
782.42164'0268—dc20
[E]
93-20627 CIP AC

Published simultaneously in the United States and Canada

PRINTED IN THE UNITED STATES OF AMERICA

0 9 8 7 6 5

Bank Street Ready-to-Read™

SHE'LL BE COMING AROUND THE MOUNTAIN

by Emily Coplon, Doris Orgel, and Ellen Schecter
Illustrated by Rowan Barnes-Murphy

A Byron Preiss Book

A BANTAM BOOK
NEW YORK • TORONTO • LONDON • SYDNEY • AUCKLAND

She'll be coming
around the mountain
when she comes.
She'll be riding on the engine
when she comes.

She'll be hollering and hooting,
cows and chickens
will go scooting,
she'll be rootin'-tootin' rowdy
when she comes.

TOOT! TOOT!

She'll be driving six wild horses
when she comes.
She'll be yelling, "Hey, you horses,
let's have fun!"

YA-HOO!

They'll go bumping,
they'll go snorting,
they'll go clomping
and cavorting,
as their hoofprints spell out
"Howdy, everyone!"

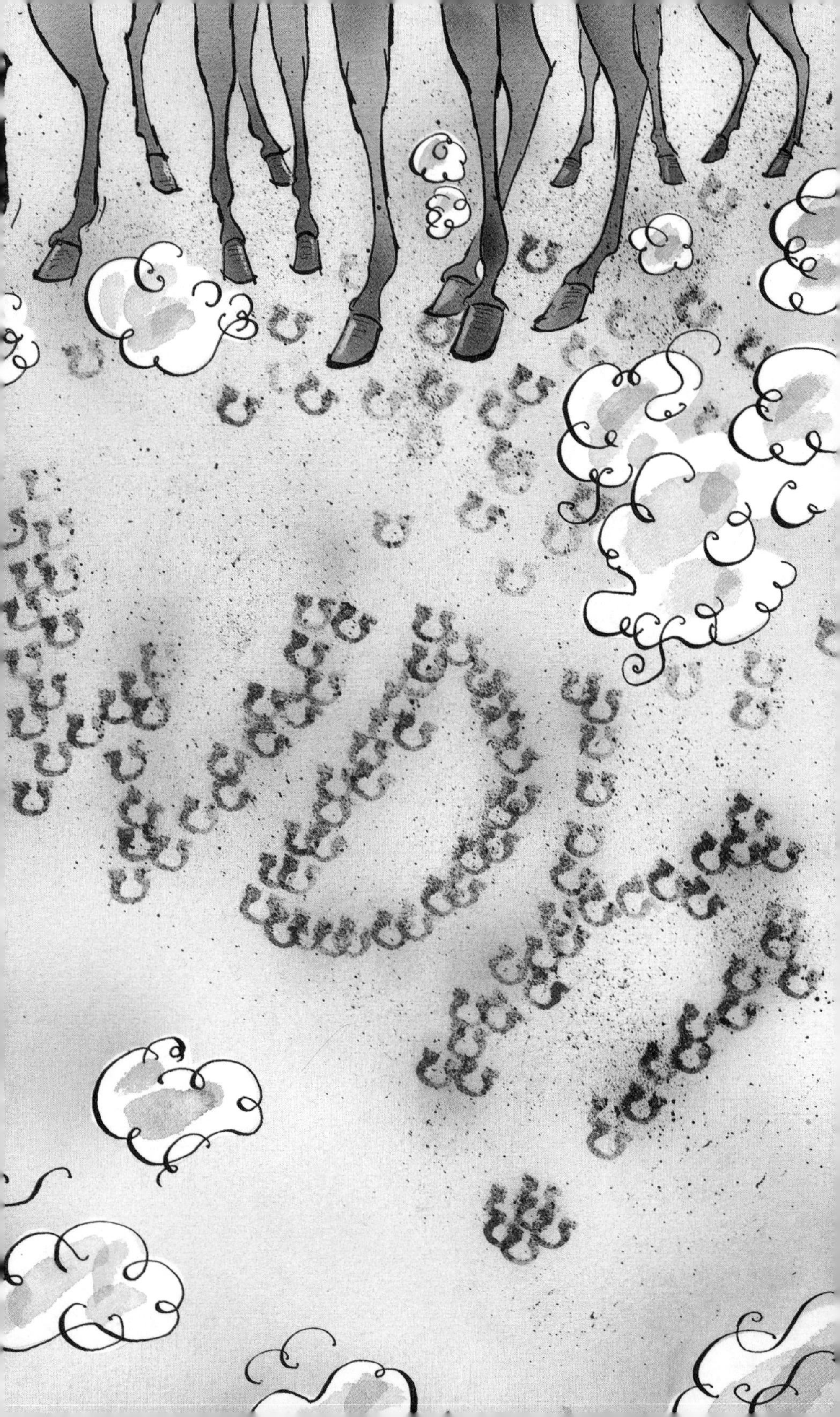

And we'll all run out to meet her
when she comes,
'cause we just can't wait
to greet her
when she comes.

Hi, BABE!

We'll wear rhinestones
and pajamas
like our papas and our mamas
for our razzle-dazzle cousin
when she comes.

Hi, CUZ!

Oh, we'll kill the old red rooster
when she comes.
And he won't crow
like he used to
when she comes.

DOODLE-DOO!

We'll eat corncob jam and chili
with a ton of piccalilli,
and we'll all have
chicken and dumplings
when she comes.

YUM!

Oh, we'll have a
bang-up hoe-down
when she comes,
do-si-do and never slow down
when she comes.

HAW!

We'll be singing
while we're dancing,
even those of us who can't sing,
and we'll do-si till we're dizzy
when she comes.

CHA!

She'll be flying six white horses
in the sky.
She'll say "Hi!"
to ten bright angels
flying by.

HIGH!

While the sun shouts
"Bye-bye, Sister!"
and the moon comes out
to kiss her,
we'll shout "Glory hallelujah!"
by and by.

BYE!

Oh, we'll all be pretty tuckered
when she's gone.
We'll be snoozing,
we'll be snoring
until dawn.

We'll be dreaming by the dozen
of our favorite kissing cousin.
Can you guess
what we'll be dreaming
when she's gone?

That she's coming
around the mountain,
here she comes!
She'll yell "Giddy-up, you horses!"
when she comes.

WHOA BACK!

Oh, we'll all run out to meet her!
Yes, we'll all run out to greet her!
And we'll all shout "Hallelujah!"
when she comes.